I0537921

Maker

Raven Johnson

Published by Raven Johnson, 2025.

MAKER

First edition. July 22, 2025.

ISBN: 979-8898601171

Written by Raven Johnson.

Table of Contents

This is for everyone who has inspired me to move forward in my dream and not to stop for anyone.

"2025 Year of the Snake - The Year of the Snake in Chinese culture is a time of quiet transformation and deep wisdom. The snake, graceful and mysterious, moves with calm purpose, reminding us of the beauty in letting go and beginning anew. Its presence invites us to shed old layers, to embrace the unknown, and to uncover the truths hidden within ourselves. Under the soft glow of lanterns, it speaks of change, reflection, and the quiet power of renewal.

Love in the Year of the Snake feels tender and profound, like a secret shared in the stillness of night. It is a year for passion and trust, where every glance and touch feels like a promise. Love flows naturally, weaving its way into our hearts with quiet strength, inviting us to see and be seen. In its embrace, we find not only another but also ourselves—a calm magic that lingers, like the whisper of a breeze beneath the stars."

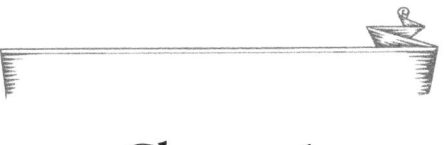

Chapter 1

The shock would have been kind as her vision became red, and the sting from the sauce was an excuse for her tears.

Lydia held her gift for her crush close to her side as she carefully wiped it off her face. She recognized the taunts and laughter from her classmates, as she had dealt with them since her freshman year.

What happened? she thought.

She wanted nothing more than to celebrate International Day with her best friend, Ichigo. It was the last time she'd spent with her friend before graduation.

Lydia knew her friend was homesick, so she made his favorites, along with her family's popular sandwiches.

"Lydia, what happened here?"

Lydia turns to find her crush and best friend, Ichigo Morimoto, standing next to the nightmare named Lamia Sinclair.

She's the popular girl, captain of the cheerleading team, leader of the debate team, rich girl, and a bona fide thot!

"It looks like Lydia loved the sauce," Lamia said with a vicious smile.

The smile alone was enough for Lydia's blood to boil as Lamia said, "Do you need a towel?"

"No thanks," Lydia said through gritted teeth.

"But it's clear that you need it," Lamia said.

Growing snickers echoed in the classroom as Ichigo jogged toward Lydia and gently took her in his arms.

The teacher arrived, and after seeing what happened, a narrowed gaze formed on his face.

"What's all the commotion?" says Mr. Star.

Lamia's face morphed into a scared girl with a slight tremble before saying, "Lydia wanted to cover me in sauce!"

"What?"

"It's true! Lydia tried to push Lamia near the balloon, but ..." said Lamia's friend before Mr. Star lifted his hand.

"We can settle this with the security camera," Mr. Star said.

"What camera?" Lamia's friend said.

"The camera I've had permission to install in this room."

"But that's impossible since there isn't one."

"Ichiro, grab my laptop."

Ichigo gently touched Lydia's back before walking to the teacher's desk and grabbing the laptop.

Once placed on a student's desk, Mr. Star typed on his laptop until revealing Lamia's lackey, replacing the glittered red balloon with one filled with sweet and sour sauce.

"This is illegal!" said Lamia's friend.

"You don't pay attention, Mr. Star asked in advance for this," Ichigo said.

A classmate quietly gave Lydia a wet cloth to clean her face in time to see Lamia's lackey rolling up in Ichigo's face.

"Just because you're the teacher's pet doesn't give you the right to..." Lamia's friend's eyes widened as she backed away from Ichigo.

"What's wrong, cat got your tongue?" Ichigo said with a daring grin.

Dang, how is he this sexy! Lydia wondered.

"Mmm, monster!"

Lydia saw literal red as she moved before Ichigo and pushed Shakeela away.

"You've got guts to call him a monster in front of me!" said Lydia.

"That's enough! Ms. Shive, we're going to the principal's office."

"Wait, it wasn't my fault, it was Lamia!"

Expressing as a worried friend, Lamia gave a convincing show, "I can't believe you would do this, Shakeela."

"You witch! You told me it would give this nerd a lesson in taking your man!"

"I've expressed my jealousy, but I would never harm someone."

"Let's go, Ms. Shive."

"No, please, I didn't do it alone."

Mr. Star had to get school security to drag her out of the classroom and follow them to the office.

Lamia slipped in between Leo and Lydia before slightly pushing Lydia away.

"I'm sorry for Shakeela's rude behavior." Lamia continued, "If you let me, I can make it up to you."

She pressed her hands on his arm and chest while blinking flirtatiously.

"Don't you have any willpower?" Lydia said.

"Who are you to lecture me, nerd?"

"A nerd with principles."

"Do you believe in the tooth fairy, too?"

Snickers echoed in the room as Lamia slapped Lydia.

"What the hell?" Lydia screamed.

"Careful, we have to be quiet. Besides, who do you think they'll believe, the daughter of the school board member or a violent nerd?"

"Oh, so you do admit it?"

"What?"

"That you don't have willpower because of your parents?"

"What?"

"Let me put it in a language your thot brain can understand: I screw guys with money."

"You bitch!"

Lydia tightened her fist when Ichiro grabbed Lamia's wrist.

"What are you doing? Let go!"

"Believe me, I'm saving your face," Ichigo said before pushing Lamia away.

"Hah, I'm Lamia Soul, what can a weak nerd do to me?"

"Try me," Lydia said.

Classmates chanted a fight when the bell rang, and the teacher next door told them to break it up, and they left with a groan.

Lamia left with a sneer, and Lydia saw Ichigo's sigh of relief.

"Dang, I wanted to rearrange her face."

"It wouldn't end with just a rearrangement, Nv Wang."

"Semantics."

"C'mon, we've got to find you another outfit."

"I don't think I can fit into your jersey."

"Are you sure?"

He moves Lydia to the corner of the classroom, "I wouldn't say it if I didn't."

Lydia felt her tongue being swallowed down her throat for a moment as Ichigo leaned close to her lips.

"Aren't you going to stop me?"

She slowly shook her head and grabbed his head before tasting nirvana.

It felt like a promised eternity tempting her to stay. She didn't know how long they had been in this position, but a clear throat from the teacher told her all she needed to know.

"It's time for lunch," Mr. Star said with a knowing grin.

Ichigo moved slowly away from her with intention, but something caught her attention.

His eyes!

It was instant, but his eyes glowed an earthly green with a hint of yellow.

"Lydia, are you okay?"

"I'm fine; I've never noticed your eyes."

"What?"

"I didn't know you had hazel eyes."

Ichigo's expression scrunched in confusion, and he shook his head.

"It's probably the light, he continues, does it bother you?"

"No, it's one of the reasons I like you."

"You... like me?"

Before she could say anything else, Mr. Star led them out of the classroom.

Lydia could've sworn her face was as red as a stop sign when they left to get his jersey.

She ignored the stares once she made it to the girls' locker room and washed the sauce off.

The rest of the day was a blur, but that moment in the classroom was etched in her mind. She knew this was her last year of high school, along with Ichigo, before going to different colleges.

If I were to reveal my love for him, why not now?

She made it to the school parking lot, and Ichigo arrived at his car.

The ride was quiet until they pulled up to her house.

"Well, thanks for the ride," she continued, "Are we still having dinner at your folks?"

"Yeah," Ichigo said with a sober expression.

"Ok, I'll see you then."

She was opening the car door when his hand softly gripped her wrist.

"Where do you think you're going?"

"I ... I was just.."

"You think you can admit to liking me without knowing the consequences?"

"Ichigo, it was a slip of the tongue, an accident."

"Well, this isn't."

He pulled her as close as possible inside his car and took what little air she had in her lungs.

ICHIGO DIDN'T KNOW what came over him at that moment, but knew it was perfect.

He had fallen in love with Lydia since she protected him from bullies in kindergarten.

The more he spent time with her, the deeper he fell, but he knew she only saw him as a friend.

When he saw her being bullied by Lamia's prank, the desire to rip her to shreds was overwhelming. But Ichigo could sense genuine bloodlust from Lydia, and with strained control, he took her in his arms.

The smell of the sweet and sour sauce, her uniqueness, had him lose his mind for a second.

But when she admitted her affection, it snapped the thin restraint in his emotions.

He wanted to devour her until all she could think of was him.

She broke away from his lips, but he softly kissed her neck until he took a nibble.

"Ichigo.."

"Mmhmm?"

"Hmm, I've never done this before and want to get married first."

He cursed under his breath at this confession as the desire magnified, but he moved away.

"Sorry, I didn't mean to..."

He kissed her lush lips and said, "Thanks for telling me, but I can't do this."

The hurt in her dark brown eyes broke him when she moved away.

"Then I guess we can forget this ever happened."

"No, I can't do this without making you officially mine."

Lydia widened her eyes and said, "What do you mean?"

"If I'm going to have you, I want all of you."

Lydia's eyes widened, "You mean..."

"I want to marry you."

"But we're still kids."

"Not now, but someday, until then, will you be my girlfriend?"

"I'm not dreaming?"

He chuckled and said, "If it is, it's a shared one."

Lydia softly kissed him and said, "I'll be your girlfriend."

After kissing her goodbye, he thanked the lucky stars for this chance and drove home.

AS HE WENT INSIDE HIS home, he noticed the subtle changes his mother was making for the Chinese New Year.

The red decorations were laid out near the den with different versions of tigers.

A 5'2 middle-aged Asian woman with brown eyes and long hair exited the kitchen with a concerned expression.

"Ichigo, what happened? You didn't answer your phone?"

"I was busy, Mom."

"Were you hanging out with Lydia again?"

"Yeah, I dropped her off today."

"Is she okay?"

"We had a problem during class, but it was resolved."

His mom nodded, then moved closer to him with a piercing gaze.

Ichigo felt a stirring inside of him before a searing, burning sensation was placed on his lower side.

"It's just as I feared," his mom said.

"What is it?" he said with gritted teeth.

"My son, you've awakened the zodiac animals."

"What? No, it's not time."

"It's almost Chinese New Year, and since this mark appears, it means your mate has touched you."

"No, not yet."

"It's time for you to mate and bring harmony to your soul. She continued, So who is it?"

The pounding in his heart was a mile a minute as he knew the ramifications if they discovered Lydia.

They would strip everything from her and would be bound to him for as long as they lived. He loved her too much to have her freedom taken away.

"She's probably someone I've bumped into today."

"Then we must find her."

"What happens if I refuse to mate?"

"You have to be sent to the training grounds in Japan."

"For how long?"

"For twelve years."

He gasped from the pain and time spent away from Lydia, but knew she couldn't handle this side of him.

"That long?"

"It takes time to control the zodiac animals while fighting your urge to mate."

"How will I know who my mate is?"

"She will have the zodiac of your birth."

He knew the snake was his and immediately had to tell Lydia.

"Oh, by the way, is Lydia coming for dinner?"

He almost forgot about it, but he knew it would be the perfect time.

"Yes."

"Good, she can help with the decoration and eat."

"I'm surprised you've never allowed someone aside from me to help you."

"I like Lydia; she has a good head on her shoulders."

"I'm going to wash up."

She's our mate, don't do this!

He sighed as the zodiac animals spoke in an uproar, knowing it would be a long night.

I'm protecting her.

Bull! We're protecting her; you're running!

Shut up!

She's strong enough to take this responsibility!

No! I won't take her choice away.

A roar emerged from his mouth, shaking the house, and he refused to allow the zodiacs to control him.

I will protect her even if it kills me.

The creator's decision to make Lydia his was bittersweet, as he had to break his mate's heart.

LYDIA SMILED AT HELPING Ichiro's mother with the decorations and eating with them.

It was filled with love and warmth, especially when Ichigo's father and mother claimed her as a daughter they never had.

The first time she met them, it was a scary time because her parents were late picking her up from kindergarten. She had just met Ichigo after a small fight against bullies, so when he found out, he asked his parents to keep her company.

She thought they were going to dismiss her with their narrowed gazes, but the mother nodded with a smile. It began a growing friendship with Ichigo and the second family she came to know and love.

Honestly, she spends more time there than at home.

But her chest tightened at Ichigo's subtle distance and one-word answers.

As he parked in front of her house, she looked at his blank expression before saying, "You've been acting weird all night. What's wrong?"

He shrugged before unlocking the door, "See you later."

"Ichigo, what's going on?"

"Nothing, I just need to handle some things back home."

"What do you mean? We finished decorating for New Year's."

"I mean Japan."

The shock from his confession left a hole in her soul, but she kept her face straight.

"What's in Japan?"

"Business, since there's nothing left for me here."

Lydia grabbed a fistful of the shirt and made him look at her.

"Don't lie."

"It's the truth."

"So, you think you can toss me aside like this?"

"C'mon, Lydia, drama is not you."

"What?"

"It's been fun, but I need to focus on my future from here on out."

"You promised me that we would be together and marry someday."

Burning shame cut her as he mockingly laughed and said, "I wanted a quick lay, but it's true, a virgin is too much work."

She used every ounce of strength and slapped the smirk from his face, leaving a red palm mark.

He rose from his seat and gave her a rough kiss.

It seemed unbelievable, but the kiss was better now than before when she heard a soft tear.

"What are you doing? Stop!"

"Not yet."

"Ichigo, stop!"

He licked against her shoulder, which was more sensitive than usual, making her pant for more.

"Lydia..." He said as if in prayer.

With surprising strength, she pushed him off her and got out.

"Lydia?"

"I'm not easy,"

"You sure about that?"

She turned to look at him one last time with his long hair, small hooped earrings, lush lips, and expressive hazel oval eyes. The guy she saw, her best friend, confidant, and boyfriend, was a lie.

She walked to her house with tears and said, "Goodbye, Ichigo."

ICHIGO WATCHED WITH an inner roar of pain as Lydia walked away from him, wearing his zodiac animal on her shoulder.

He looked away as his beautiful sun slowly left him in darkness.

Staring at her gift, he slowly opened it to find a pendant of a snake in an infinity form.

Fighting the tears, he grips the pendant with a shaking fist.

"Goodbye, Lydia," he said while driving away.

Chapter 2

15 years later
Lydia sighed in enjoyment as she watched her creations being offered to the highest bidder.

"Two million dollars going once, twice... sold to paddle number 3."

She nodded with approval at the thought of acquiring new gems with this money.

Lydia's assistant, Bernie, appeared behind her and whispered, "Ms. Fierce, we must make it to the trade show before it begins."

"Of course, thanks," Lydia says as she nods to her accountant.

She left knowing that everything was in order and went to the trade show.

I hope I'll find unique gems for the spring collection, she thought.

The ride didn't last long as the car parked, and Lydia witnessed various people entering the small building.

The fireworks stall was filled with people who were preparing for the Chinese New Year celebration. It always excited her from the food to the family gatherings she would witness, a sense of belonging.

Shaking away the sudden case of homesickness, Lydia focused on the designs she planned to create during the festivity.

She decided to change into a less noticeable outfit and enter with the new visitors.

The showcases of various gems were outstanding and could easily be included with her designs.

She found a few diamonds, emeralds, rubies, but knew something was missing.

"Hey there, miss, would you be interested in these gems?"

She turned to find a seller who seemed young in this business, but decided to check it out.

The gems were too beautiful and rare for a standard trade show.

"Aren't you sure that you're in the right trade show?"

"I'm exactly where I need to be, Miss."

Lydia stared at the seller before carefully choosing a rainbow-colored gem that refreshed and brightened her soul.

"I'll choose this one."

"Ah, wise choice, this gem is said to bring the bearer good fortune."

"I don't believe in luck," Lydia said as her assistant placed the gem with the others.

"I assure you, it brings good fortune."

Lydia smiled before taking out her wallet and said, "How much does it cost?"

"It's on the house."

"I'm sorry?"

"It's my privilege to serve the queen."

Queen?

Lydia stares at her assistant's frown before saying, "I'm not royalty."

The vendor tilted his head before winking and said, "Of course, my mistake."

"How much?"

The vendor offered a price that is seriously a steal, but she decided not to tempt fate.

The vendor received the payment and gave a blessing before meeting with another customer.

"Your mother wants you to call her," said Bernie.

"I'll call her once I'm finished."

"Of course."

"What else?"

"The company wants to know about your next creation to get the ball rolling for the coming season."

"Tell them I'll send the sketches tomorrow."

"Yes, Ms. Fierce."

"Thank you, Bernie."

"It's my privilege."

"No, it's mine. How about we go to the corner store to get something to eat?"

"As a friend, I have no idea why you would still go to an old shack."

Lydia chuckled before saying, "Because they have the best wings in town."

"You're a millionaire."

"And?"

"There are many fine restaurants upstate."

"Are you coming or not?"

"I'll get the burger."

Lydia smiled. Bernie loosened his tie before following her to the car.

"It's almost Chinese New Year, Ms. Fierce."

"I know."

"Are you still going to visit Mr and Mrs. Morimoto?"

She couldn't help but smile at the loving atmosphere the couple carries with each visit.

But as always, the pain of Ichigo's rejection still stung even after so many years.

I'm glad he's running a business overseas so that I won't see his handsome face. Dang, focus, Lydia!

"Yes, I promised Mrs. Morimoto a piece of jewelry for the holiday."

"Is it from last season?"

"Nah, this one will be under wraps."

Lydia stared at the rainbow stone that would be perfect for the family.

"I'll hold off the calls until you've finished."

She nodded before leaving the building, not knowing someone was following her every step.

"WE'VE GOT EVERYTHING ready for the festival," a servant said.

"Good, it's going to plan," a masked man said.

"What about the jeweler?"

The masked man continued to sharpen his blade as he said, "Leave her to me."

"She has the zodiac jewel."

"Do I need to repeat myself?"

The servant bowed before saying, "Forgive me."

"Leave."

The servant disappeared into the darkness as the masked man sheathed his sword.

Jeweler, prepare to meet your maker, he thought, as he followed his target.

He had been chosen to guard the jewel, but by some trickery, it disappears on his watch.

Luckily, his soul was currently connected to the jewel and knew its location.

He was given a picture and location of the jeweler, but couldn't help but be mesmerized by her eyes. It brought his zodiac tattoo to life, threatening his human form before transforming into an animal.

The jeweler shouldn't have had such an effect on him, but he had an idea that brought a fanged smile.

I'm coming for you.

ONCE LYDIA FINISHED her business with delicious wings and bid Bernie goodbye, she returned home to form her project.

She could picture her next creations entering the workplace in the back and working on a few pieces.

She knew Mrs. Morimoto loved the Chinese New Year and embedded the chosen jewel into a masterpiece.

It took some maneuvering, but the results were breathtaking. The diamonds reflect the scales of the snake, rubies for the eyes, and the rainbow jewel embedded in the center of its tail.

Flawless!

After placing her creation inside a small red box, she got ready for bed.

The steaming, hot shower was perfect for her muscles, but she knew she had to finish one more thing before sleeping.

Grabbing her cell phone, she dialed a number and heard it ring for a couple of seconds before it answered.

"Hey, Lydia, sweetheart."

"Hey, Mom, everything ok?"

"Oh, I'm fine. I wanted to know if you could come for dinner tomorrow."

She checked her calendar and found the date empty.

"I'll be able to come."

"Perfect, I've got a surprise for you."

She inwardly groaned and said, "Mom, it's not another surprise guest, is there?"

"No."

"Mom -"

"Baby, you've promised you'll start dating this year."

Stupid tequila

"I am."

"Oh?"

"Yes, ma'am."

"Bring him over for dinner."

"What?"

"I mean it, Lydia Rain Fierce, bring him or face my surprise."

The dial tone was deafening as her tired mind went into overdrive.

She placed her phone on the charger and slid into the silk bed sheets, futilely trying to calm her thoughts.

It didn't help her case since she hadn't given the opposite sex a chance to get to know her, due to having a tight schedule.

She always manages to attract ass-holes who are interested in one-night stands, wanting to string unsuspecting women along. The annoyance from dipping into the dating pool was enough for her to drown voluntarily.

The guys in her neck of the woods were old perverts, married cheaters, or straight-up boys. It's a problem when the good ones seem snatched up without notice.

An idea occurred to her as she grabbed her phone and dialed.

"Hello?" said a groggy Bernie.

"It's me."

"Yes, Ms. Fierce?"

"Cut the sarcasm; I need a favor."

"What is it?"

"I need you to be my stand-in boyfriend."

The silence alone was enough, but the laughter raked her nerves.

"Bernie, quiet!"

"Sorry, Boss, but I like being married."

"I'll make it worth your while."

"We're listening," said Bernie's wife, Gabriella.

"Hey Gab..."

"Cut the crap, how much?"

"Bonus of five hundred."

"Make it a thousand, and you've got a deal."

"You're considering this?" Bernie said in disbelief.

"Babe, it's a free dinner, and we can replace the couch."

"It's a good couch."

"Not since Rufus made it his favorite scratch post."

"I don't know..."

Lydia chuckled at the couple's banter when hearing the four magic words from Bernie, "Fine, I'll do it."

"Thank you, you won't regret it."

"Too late, good night."

She hung up in relief and breathed a sigh of relief that everything was finally going to plan.

THE MASKED MAN ENTERED the jeweler's house with little effort as he searched for the zodiac jewel.

He tilts his head, bombarded by the jeweler's scent, before walking into a station.

A certain glow emanated from a small box, pulsing the closer he came. It was familiar yet promising as he took the box into his hand and then opened it. The intricate diamond detail of the snake was outstanding, but at its center lay the jewel.

She's going to suffer for this!

The mere boldness to place something sacred with metal made him growl.

With the jewel in his possession, he went inside the bedroom, claws sharpening to tear.

The jeweler's scent was more potent than before, driving him to insanity, but he focused on the task.

The claws were near her throat when a pain shook him, knowing where it came from.

What's the meaning of this?

Have you lost your mind?

She has stolen our sacred treasure.

Do not touch her!

What has this woman done to my animals?

He had come to an understanding with his animals years ago, but now it seems like the first year in training.

The training was brutal, but he had somehow managed to survive it. However, since the problem stemmed from this woman and how his animals reacted, he concluded that she was a witch.

I'll have her break it, but time is running short, and my kingdom needs me.

The masked man sheathed his claws and tightened his fist.

I have no choice.

He pressed his hand against the jeweler's mouth as the person's eyes opened and narrowed.

Interesting

The jeweler struggled before he whispered, "You fight me, I'll end you."

He holds his hand as the jeweler tries to bite him and kicks amusingly on his chest.

The masked man grabs her legs before maneuvering around and tying her up.

"Let me go!" the jeweler said.

"You've committed a grave mistake."

"No, you did,"

She twisted out of his grasp and headbutted under his chin.

"What the —"

She barely moved away, but with a growl, he grabbed her shirt, revealing her shoulder.

The gleam of the snake tattoo glows with velocity and power.

"No," the masked man said with gritted teeth.

"Let me go!"

The zodiac animals he had controlled for so long emerged from their slumber as they spoke through his mouth.

"Never again."

He took out a rag filled with enhanced chloroform and covered her mouth. She struggled against him for a moment longer until her body went limp.

The masked man placed her firmly against his body as if another part of him had fused back together.

Seeing her face and smelling her scent brought a stabbing pain to his mind, but he focused on the task at hand.

"It's time to rectify your mistake," he whispered in her ear before leaving the house with her in his arms.

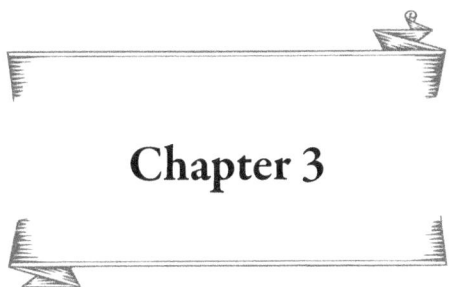

Chapter 3

She didn't know how long she had been unconscious, but judging from the soft light coming from the window, it was late afternoon.

The grogginess was not fun, especially when her situation involved a kidnapping into an unknown location.

Lydia felt the rough texture of the rope against her wrists and legs as she looked for anything in the room to use as a way to cut herself loose.

The room was arranged uniquely and felt tranquil, but it didn't help her mind.

She found a golden hair ornament on a red oak dresser and scooted enough until reaching it with her toes.

The door revealed a petite female in a red-flowered kimono carrying a serving table filled with various foods. She laid the food down on the bed and turned to leave.

"Hey, can you help me?"

The servant looked at her, scared, before skittering away and closing the door.

"Hey, wait, help a sister out!"

Lydia cursed as she maneuvered the hairpin until it was in her hands.

The doors opened, revealing the kidnapper wearing a red monster's mask with a samurai sword on his hip.

"Do you know the consequences of your crime?" said the kidnapper.

"I can ask you the same since abduction is an offense."

The kidnapper chuckled at her comment, which fueled her anger, and said, "It could be if someone is looking for you."

"Where did you take me?"

"Why? Planning to escape?"

Lydia refused to answer that question and said, "No, I want to take in the sights."

She noticed his tightened grip on his sword, bringing a smile to her lips.

"Aren't you afraid?"

Lydia huffed in disbelief, "No, should I be?"

An unnatural growl emanated from him, leaving a shiver down her spine, but she lifted her head higher.

"I can easily kill you for theft of the zodiac jewel."

Zodiac Jewel?

"Whatever gems or jewels I acquire, it's completely legit."

The sound of the unsheathed dagger from his boot heightened the fight-or-flight response, and his advanced steps encouraged her to finish cutting through the binds.

"Don't make me laugh."

He raised his arm in time as Lydia freed her binds to dodge the attack, resulting in a damaged mattress and a deep cut on his arm.

She can imagine the expression behind the mask and said, "I might die today, but you'll remember this."

"Why you..."

"I ain't going down without a fight!"

She expected the guy to kill her instantly, but surprisingly, he laughed and said, "You're truly entertaining."

The wound she inflicted was healing before her eyes.

Oh crap!

"Just kill me."

"No."

He moved fast, and before she knew it, the binds on her legs disappeared.

"What do you want?"

He revealed the box, inheriting the jewelry made for Mrs. Morimoto, and said, "Who gave you the zodiac jewel?"

"It was a vendor from the trade show."

"Anything else?"

"He was five-one in height, wearing a green shrouded hood."

The kidnapper cursed and slammed his hand against the wall. It made her wonder if he was part of a growing cult that belonged in a padded room.

"So, it was him."

"What?"

"Nevertheless, it's time to fix what you've broken."

"What I've broken!?"

She moved on autopilot, grabbed the box from his grasp, and said, "You're a kidnapper and a thief, so don't accuse me of destruction of property."

"Why should I believe you?"

"The evidence is clearly in your hands, so why don't you see for yourself?"

"No wait!"

Lydia opened the box and watched as the jewelry came to life, slithering around her neck as a necklace.

A force echoed from within and out, pushing the kidnapper against the wall hard.

A rainbow afterglow surrounded her before disappearing, leaving her in disbelief.

"What the heck!"

A groan from the man caught her attention, and she found his damaged mask lying nearby.

As the dust settled, she saw the face that had haunted her for the past fifteen years.

"It can't be... Ichigo?"

He slowly opened his eyes before narrowing them and said, "Do you know what you've just done, Jeweler?"

He doesn't remember me?

"Enlighten me, jackass."

"You've made yourself a target."

"How? I'm stuck in God knows where, and you've got the guts to treat me this way," she continued, "Haven't you done enough in my life?"

"What are you talking about?"

"Stop playing with me, Ichigo."

He quickly grabbed her by the throat and said, "How do you know my name?"

"I won't forget the face of a traitor!"

"Don't flatter yourself, woman."

He pushes her back on the damaged bed before jumping on top of her. She stared at him to find his eyes like a tiger's and quickly moved her attention to his lips.

What's the matter with me?

She relived her last encounter with his lips when he said, "You're just a witch that's manipulating me. You're not my mate!"

"You're nuts! What are you talking about?"

"Don't lie!"

The roar echoed around the room and the earth, but she knew it was all an interrogation tactic.

"Ichigo, you know me; I don't lie."

He moved closer for her to smell his scent of Sandalwood and vanilla, which, after all these years, drove her crazy.

"Are you delusional as well?"

"Forget you, Ichigo, let me go!"

"Who is your leader?"

"Let go of me."

She struggled to get away from him, and when he grabbed her nightshirt, a tear could be heard.

"What are you doing?"

He took hold of the necklace but cursed as it didn't budge, cutting his hand.

The blood landed on the necklace, touching her skin. Immediately, the tattoo on her shoulder was on fire, bringing images of a snake wrapping itself around her and Ichigo.

A burning sensation coursed through her, bringing tears to her eyes as it increased until it ebbed.

She felt herself dropping to the floor when a pair of strong arms caught her in time. Lydia looked up to find a confused Ichigo as he placed her against his chest.

The feeling of being in his arms left her warm, but his cold eyes removed any trace of safety.

"It's impossible, I already have a woman," he whispered in disbelief.

"Congratulations, I can't wait to meet her," Lydia said sarcastically.

"How did you acquire this marking?"

"I don't know."

"Confess!"

"I told you I don't know; it appeared after you left me!"

After he left, she dealt with the bullies and her parents when they discovered a snake tattoo on her shoulder.

Despite her telling them the truth, they didn't believe her and tried to remove it without success.

"I've never seen you in my life."

Lydia refused to be bothered by his words, even as they cut more deeply than a knife.

"Fine, then if you don't know me, get rid of my tattoo."

He looked away from her, ashamed of this predicament, "I... can't."

"Listen, you're married. It should be simple for you."

Ichigo's hands covered her upper arms and said, "I haven't married yet. Once my blood touched your skin and the jewel, it's forever."

He might as well have slapped her then; it would've been a good excuse to kick him where it hurts.

"So you mean we're stuck like this?"

"Yes."

She slapped his hands off of her, jumped from his arms, and glared at him.

"I refuse to be stuck in this mumbo jumbo crap, especially with you."

He moved away in surprise before saying, "Fine, I'll find the wise man; he'll know how to settle this."

"Good, besides, your wife wouldn't approve."

"Not wife, mate."

He rubbed his eyes before sitting on the ruined bed.

"I don't see a ring on your finger, so it means you are cheating."

"She's my future queen of the zodiac, so hold your tongue, or I'll do it for you."

"I'm so scared. Listen, call your wise man so I can return to civilization, ok, flapjack?"

"What did you call me?"

"Flapjack, or don't you understand insults?"

"I'm warning you, hold your tongue."

Lydia stepped up to him with a boldness that shocked her as she said, "Make me."

ICHIGO HAD NEVER MET a more infuriating woman or a more beautiful one. The challenge from her dark brown eyes, voluptuous body, and brown skin made it hard for him to concentrate. But the direct rebellion from her snapped something inside and brought her soft body against his hard one.

"Say that again."

She moved her face closer without breaking eye contact and said, "Make... me, Morimoto."

He slanted his mouth against hers as the desire to tame this witch covered his mind. The taste brought a moan from his throat as she returned his kiss with ferocity.

The taste of her lips reminded him of the sweet berries of this land, and he wanted to drown in it.

Ichigo cursed the timing as the Chinese New Year had already begun, and it was only a matter of time before his enemies knew this circumstance.

Focus on our mate, the zodiac animals said.

She isn't our mate!

This woman is our mate and not a witch!

He couldn't believe even his animals were against him and clouding his mind with lust.

Ichigo roamed his hand around her body as he couldn't get enough while pressing her against his desire.

"Ichigo!" she gasped.

He kissed her neck towards the tattoo, making both bodies sing in euphoria. "I'll make you confess."

He hissed as she licked over his chest and gave a bite.

With ease, he removed her clothes and groaned at the view of flesh displayed before him.

"I don't have anything to tell you."

He moved his lips to her bosom and took a nipple into his mouth as she gasped.

I'm going to make you confess, witch.

It felt like he was convincing himself as he continued to ravage her fruitlessly, trying to ignore his growing desire.

"Your majesty, I have great news, oh!" a servant said.

Ichigo cursed at the timing as this witch stiffened in his arms before struggling to get out of his grasp.

The servant bowed and said, "Forgive me, I didn't know."

He released her and blocked the servant's gaze as the jeweler covered herself.

"What is it?" Ichigo said with a growl.

"It's the land, it has been made whole."

"Impossible, only my mate could heal it."

"Nevertheless, your majesty, the kingdom is alive again."

He nodded and waved the servant away, then frowned at the woman.

"What witchcraft you've done?"

The jeweler had the nerve to laugh in his face before saying, "I don't touch that poison, your highness."

"I will find out soon enough, Wiseman!"

The Wiseman appeared within the second, and he watched the jeweler's expression of shock.

"Yes, your majesty?"

"Look into her soul and uncover her deceit."

The Wiseman bowed and then moved closer to the woman, but she moved away in fear.

A warning growl came from his throat as the Wiseman said, "Rest assured, I won't harm her."

"What are you going to do?" the jeweler said.

"Simple, look into my eyes."

"No way."

"You won't feel a thing."

The narrowed gaze sent to the wise man was enough to freeze even his soul, but she nodded.

"Fine, if it'll prove this guy wrong."

Chapter 4

S he felt lost in this guy's black gaze until she woke up in a golden throne room. "Where am I?"

"You're in the throne room of the zodiac."

"I thought you were going to read my mind?"

"Oh, that was done a second ago." "I needed to talk with you."

"What's to talk about other than you selling a jewel that cost me my freedom?"

"I have a good explanation."

"Oh? Did you tell him, I'm not a thief or witch?"

"Of course."

"Then release me now!"

She thought she was going to fight her way out, but to her surprise, the man bowed low.

"Please forgive me, but it was the only way for his majesty's true mate, you, to appear."

"What is this, mate, business and Ichigo being king?"

The Wiseman raised his head and answered, "The Ichigo you've known in the past is the rightful ruler of the zodiac kingdom."

"Ruler?"

"Yes, and since Ichigo hadn't united with you after twelve years of training, his memory of you waned."

"He said that he already has a mate, so how is this possible?"

"The woman he claims as his mate is an impostor."

"How do you know?"

He revealed the jewel she bought from him and blew on it. The jewel itself separates into twelve crystals, and by light, it shows the zodiac animals.

"The jewel reveals the integrity of the person and true mates of the zodiac clan."

Disbelief coursed through her mind at how Ichigo's treatment of her ended their friendship.

"He doesn't want me, so why the fuss?"

"His Highness is in danger, and mating with you will save him."

"He doesn't remember me, and I'm not a prostitute."

"I mean no disrespect; please save him."

"I can't help someone who doesn't want it. Anyway, I've got to get back to my life."

"What if I could promise a safe travel home?"

Lydia crossed her arms and saw his genuine expression. "What do you mean?"

"If you would prove to him that you're here to help and not harm, then complete the mating, you can go home."

"Why are you so determined?"

Not even my parents liked the idea of my friendship with Ichigo.

"Because he is like a brother I've never had, and since he took his place as king, he made the kingdom a safer place to live."

"Why can't his parents take back the throne?"

The wise man shook his head in sadness, "Since his parents left the realm, they have forgotten it except for the lineage of zodiac animals and mates."

Lydia felt sad for the people who had lost their homes, but with their determination to make a home, it became a haven for her and others.

"How far am I from home?"

"Not far, you'll need to get a flight."

"What is this place?"

"This is the Zhi hue kingdom, another realm."

"Realm?"

"Yes, this is the land of the zodiac shifters."

Lydia chuckled but saw the serious expression on the Wiseman and groaned.

"If you're shifters, why the human disguise?"

"We're naturally human, but it's in the bloodline."

"Do the spirits of the zodiac animals pick each person?"

"More or less, we become the zodiac animal."

"How can you tell?"

"By our tattoos."

"Ichigo's a freaking snake!?"

She shuddered at the image of Ichigo being a slithering serpent.

"Yes, but as king, he can be any animal of the zodiac."

"Convenient."

"Burdensome."

She couldn't understand why he didn't tell her this when they were friends.

"Why didn't he tell me this?"

"I'm afraid you'll have to ask his majesty."

"How can I do that if he can't remember me?"

"Once he spends time with you, it will resurface his memories."

The possibility of him remembering their last encounter wasn't appealing.

"Sorry, but I don't desire to recall my heartbreak."

"It's been twelve years, things have changed for his majesty."

"Listen, I'm not the same little girl with a heart on her sleeve. This woman has her throne."

"I don't know what happened between you two, but please allow me to help."

"What can you do?"

"I can allow you to see what he's done for the past 15 years."

She wanted to reject, but her heart, that pesky organ, wanted to know.

"Sure, when can you do it?"

"Once you've helped him."

"Deal, so where's the door to get out of this realm?"

"It's a bridge and can only be used by the king."

Dang!

"What can I do?"

"You need to marry."

"What!?"

"It'll show unity to the people."

"Feels like a shotgun wedding."

"Be assured it's only temporary."

"But what about this mate, he already has?"

"Since His Majesty and you united your markings, the kingdom acknowledges you."

"Even though I'm..."

"Human?"

"Black."

"Hah, we look at the soul."

She slowly nodded and said, "Ok, what's the second requirement?"

"To help find the cause of our majesty's declining power."

"You're the Wiseman; surely you can find out."

"Normally, I would, but there's an unknown barrier in my way."

"So the reason the realm is back to normal..."

"Your presence and unification with his majesty activated the jewel, healing the land."

"But he's still weak?"

"Once the cause is dealt with, you'll see why he's the king."

I won't be around if I can help it.

"Alright, and third?"

"Oh, it's simple, have sex with him."

She couldn't stop the heat from her cheeks if she wanted to in this moment.

"For a Wiseman, you're blunt."

"I wasn't always the wise man, and believe me, I know more than you'll ever learn."

He wasn't any older than nineteen at best, but the sage look in his eyes spoke years of wisdom.

"I'll gladly find the cause of his weakness and work on the other two later."

"Of course, and thank you, my queen."

The Wiseman bowed as Lydia said, "Stop calling me, queen!"

Before raising her voice at the Wiseman, she gasped for air, opening her eyes to the bed with the golden hairpin in her hand.

Lydia looked around, seeing the room was bigger and grander than the last.

She looked down to find herself in a new outfit, soft to the touch, with the colors of purple and gold. Touching gave a certain calm until something felt missing.

The necklace! How the hell did the wiseman get it off of me?

She shook her head.

"Focus, I need to find out what's causing Ichigo to be weak," Lydia murmured.

With the plan in mind, she placed the braids in a cute bun and secured the pin to hold it in place.

Looking at the typical places, she couldn't find anything screaming absorbent of power.

I could search the grounds and find better clues.

With a plan in mind, she opens the door to find a soldier wearing ancient armor blocking her way out.

"Excuse me; I need to see Ichigo."

The soldier glanced at her and answered, "His Majesty is busy; he'll return in a moment."

"Can you get him?"

"His Majesty ordered me to protect you until he returns."

Perfect, meaning I can't go anywhere.

She was about to commit an escape when her traitorous stomach decided to make itself known.

The guard stared at her with a raised eyebrow and said, "I'll summon your maid."

"Wait, I don't have a maid."

"Just relax, your grace."

She closed the door, wanting to curse a storm in the room, but did a few breathing exercises.

The opening of the door led her to see not Ichigo but the same maid who had run from Lydia.

She was a humble beauty, her skin as pale as marble, with a soft, gentle atmosphere.

The girl bowed as she said, "Greetings, my queen, how may I serve you?"

"Where am I?"

The girl frowned at the question and said, "You're in Japan, my lady."

Japan!?

"Which part?"

"Tokyo, my lady."

I'm going to murder that king, but first, I need to check out the palace.

Lydia glanced at the girl and said, "What's your name?"

"Chika, your majesty."

"Can you cut the majesty? But first, we need to have a clear understanding."

"Yes?"

"Simply call me, Lydia."

Her shocked expression was comical, but Lydia kept the smile to herself.

"I refuse to disrespect my queen."

This is harder than I thought.

"Ok, then how about you address me as a friend privately?"

"I don't know."

"Relax, do I have to make it an order?"

A small smile crept onto Chika's face, and she shook her head.

"Good, now. Is it possible for me to see the palace?"

"Of course, allow me to request it from his highness?"

More like jackassness

"Sure."

It didn't take long for permission to be granted, and even less time to receive a warning to stay close to the palace.

The tour was grander than she had thought, as the maid guided her through a grand library the size of what she imagined Alexandria, a kitchen with various delicious foods, inner family rooms, and the botanical gardens.

People and zodiac animals roamed in harmony, reminding her of the serenity of Nirvana.

Lydia noticed a crowd and moved toward them when Chika appeared before her.

"Please, my lady, his majesty forbade us to move from the palace."

Lydia saw Chika's slight tremble, but her eyes were resolute.

"Chika, don't worry, you're here with me and the bodyguard."

"But -"

"It's near the garden, and I want to see the people."

"Very well, but take this just in case."

She gave Lydia a jade ring and followed her as the people prepared to view the fireworks.

She sensed the guard who blocked her way to freedom behind them.

Sweet blossoms enveloped her senses as the silver moon lighted the land with a mystical glow.

Booms of fireworks in the shape of each zodiac animal were displayed until the animal of the year, the snake, was given the grandest spotlight. The people were celebrating as expected for the Chinese New Year; the children's laughter made her smile.

Staring at the firework snake brought warmth to her shoulder, and she wondered if Ichigo had the same sensation.

It was pleasant until sudden gravity took her down to the ground, and her screams echoed across the place. She rose to find the guard holding his arm covered in blood as the attacker descended its weapon over the guard.

"No, stop!" Lydia said.

The rainbow aura showered over her before striking the assailant across the garden.

Another assailant appeared from the darkness and said, "Kill her."

Lydia pushed Chika out of the way into the pond and joined her as more assassins swung their swords. She freaked out once she discovered how deep it was, but sensed a calmness as she glided effortlessly across it with Chika following.

"Where is she?" the leader said.

Lydia found a place where they couldn't find her or Chika, but close enough to witness. A rumble shook her feet as murmurs of fear from the assassins became audible when Ichigo appeared with glowing eyes.

"It's the king; now's our chance!" said the leader.

Before the assassin could strike, He brutally annihilated him without a backward glance. She saw something golden slither behind him, revealing two intimidating Ophiophagus Hannah King cobras that surrounded Ichigo before striking each assassin, save for the leader.

"This isn't over; we will rule this world," the leader said before vanishing as the snakes struck.

Lydia watched in amazement as the snakes gradually decreased in size until they fused to Ichigo's hip into tattoos.

Once it was over, she had a better view of Ichigo's well-honed body. The moon shined in a way that she couldn't help but pay attention to his six pack and muscles a curvy woman can hold on to for a while.

Mentally shaking her head, she looked at Chika and said, "Are you okay?"

"I'm alright, milady."

"Didn't I tell you that you'll be hunted?" a familiar whisper caressed her ear.

Lydia turned around to find Ichigo glaring before picking her up and over his shoulder.

"Put me down!"

"No."

THIS WOMAN IS UNBELIEVABLE! he thought.

He carried her across the pond as the maid followed with a bowed head.

"Put me down, bastard!"

Despite the gasps from his subjects, he tried to keep his mouth from smirking.

"You'll be with me."

"I told you I'm innocent! Put me down."

He didn't know why, but he wanted to believe her. Ever since apprehending her, images of a younger version of this woman have been invading his thoughts.

Whenever he tried to delve into his memories, flaming pain interfered.

At least I know she's not a witch.

The Wiseman told him this much, saying she was the destined mate and queen of the Zhi hue kingdom.

He knows that an explanation will be given to his chosen mate, but first, the need to tame this woman is at the top of the list.

"Maid!" he roared.

"Yes, your Highness," the maid said, bowing.

Ichigo glared at her and said, "Arrange for the seamstresses."

"Yes, Your Majesty."

"Don't allow anyone to enter my chambers; I need to speak with the *queen*."

"Yes, Your Majesty."

"Excuse me, but I'm still here, and her name is *Chika*."

He ignored the woman's protests as he lugged her to his bedchambers.

The journey from the garden to the chambers was a nightmare as his hand roamed against her plush brown skin.

Once inside, he ordered the woman's maid to stay outside and instructed a new guard to be posted so they would not be disturbed.

He dumped her on the bed and moved away to clear the lust clouding his mind.

"Ichigo, I have a right to stay in my room until this nightmare ends."

How does she know my name?

"Who sent you?"

"No one, besides, aren't you supposed to be doing royal duties?"

"You haven't answered my question."

"NO ... ONE!!"

The woman's yell shook the earth, he sighed as yells of fear could be heard outside, and he decided on a different strategy.

He was transfixed as the rainbow aura flowed around her, transforming her brown eyes into green.

How is it possible without the jewel?

"What's your name?"

Her sorrowful expression tore at him as she said, "Lydia Fierce."

"Lydia," he said slowly.

Immediately, an ache pierced his mind as her name echoed through it. Soft hands touched his back, and he turned to find Lydia rubbing his back.

"What are you doing?"

"Helping."

"This isn't proper!"

"Even now, your mental britches are too tight. I was your best friend."

"I don't remember you. Doesn't that disturb you?"

"Compared to what you did last time, this is easy to swallow."

He turned to stare at her and said, "What do you mean by your best friend?"

Lydia moved her hands against a tight spot, which made him inwardly groan as she answered, "You ended our friendship and..."

"And what?"

She shook her head, "Nothing, you left, and I never saw you again until you kidnapped me."

"I didn't tell you why?"

"Other than me being difficult to take to bed."

He flinched at her icy response and watched as her eye color returned to normal.

"I see."

"Is that all?"

"No."

She moved in his face with narrowed eyes and said, "You're hiding something, what is it?"

"Stop."

"No, I don't give a crap if you're the king of Siam, you're answering my question."

"How are you, my mate?" Ichigo roared, amazed as she didn't move a muscle.

"I wish I could tell you, since I never had sex with you."

"What?"

"Nope, you wanted to honor and marry before having all of me."

The tattoos glowed as an image of him staring intensely into a younger Lydia's eyes as that vow flowed from his lips.

"Did you give yourself away?"

He held his breath as she smiled. He imagined the perfect torture for the man who took her innocence.

"Despite it being the twenty-first century, I chose not to waste my time with sex."

His lust thundered to life at her admission as he slowly touched her face.

"Why? It's natural for the flesh to desire."

She moved from his touch and crossed her arms.

"I choose the self-discipline before fleeting wants."

He followed her retreat before sniffing as her scent enveloped him like a cloak and, before knowing it, kissed her.

His manhood grew enlarged as she returned his kiss as if claiming him.

Why is this more familiar?

Ichigo wouldn't allow the mate that he had picked to touch him in any way. And when necessary, he fought hard against the zodiac animals inside him as revulsion took hold of him when touching her.

But with this woman, it was like breathing, refusing to live without it again in this lifetime.

In the beginning, she fought as he tried to devour her, but at this moment, she was like a siren calling him to her territory.

With ease, Ichigo had Lydia in front of him before moving her closer, smelling her desire.

Growling, he turned Lydia around, letting her feel his manhood, bringing a moan from her.

Her generous butt seems to cushion him; he wants to do nothing but tear off her clothes and feast.

It felt like heaven until hearing the sounds of hell in the form of a screech coming from behind the doors.

"Please don't come in, his majesty ordered not to be disturbed," the maid said.

"I'm the chosen mate of the King; I demand entrance," the woman shrieked.

Ichigo cursed as Lydia moved away from him and leaned against the wall.

"Wait, you can't —"

"Silence or I'll have your tongue ripped out."

Immediately, the doors slammed open to reveal a beautiful, red-haired woman wearing a jade kimono, a fashionably styled black-haired bun, and lovely features enhanced by subtle makeup. But it didn't help as her almond-shaped eyes narrowed in fury as she looked at the display of what had transpired.

"I thought I said no one is to enter except for the seamstresses?"

The maid and the guard ran inside, bowing, and said, "Forgive us."

"I'll deal with you later. Leave us."

As they left and closed the door, he stared at the woman who had interrupted his time with Lydia.

"What brings you, my lady?" Ichigo asked as his tattoos aggravated his skin.

"Who is this *queen* whom the Wiseman deemed worthy?"

"Yeah, that's me," Lydia said, standing beside him.

He saw her stiffen as she stared at his ordained mate and asked, "Lydia, what is it?"

"Of all the chicks on earth, you chose her?"

"Of course, she was my first choice."

"It's nice to see you again, Lydia," his ordained mate said with a slight bow.

"I don't return the pleasantries, Lamia."

Chapter 5

If she could think of various scenarios, it wouldn't be this one.

Lamia tilted her head, looking at Ichigo and Lydia with a sneer.

"It's lovely to see you again," Lamia said.

"Can't say the same," Lydia said.

She knew the tension was thicker in the room as the guard stared at Ichigo's eyes without movement.

Ichigo nodded his head, allowing the poor guy to close the doors.

"How do you know Lamia?" Ichigo said.

Seriously!

Lydia crossed her arms and said, "Old classmates."

Ichigo frowned and moved his gaze to Lydia, "That's impossible. I've known her all my life, and she has never mentioned you."

"I'm not surprised since you don't remember me."

"I can't help but see that this dear woman *has* a *mental* ill*ness*," Lamia said, smiling.

Lydia desired nothing more than to have the heifer's hair in her grasp, but noticed a darkness around the woman. Carefully, she paid attention until it moved from her back to her lips.

She watches as Lamia moves closer to Ichigo with obvious intent, which makes her blood boil at her boldness.

Lydia moves until she stands beside Leo, making Lamia pause, and says, "This mentally ill woman is your *queen* and will do well to remember that."

"I've yet to see his mark on you."

Lamia placed her finger on his chest and lightly roamed. Lydia glanced at Ichigo, noticing his slight smirk as if daring her to do something.

Lydia rolled her eyes but grabbed Lamia's hand, touching his chest, and twisted it until it was behind her back.

"Let me go!"

"You're hard of hearing; I said I'm your queen, which means the king is off limits."

"I'm still his chosen mate."

Lydia grinned as she tightened her hold on the woman's hand, knowing it was painful.

"I'll read the laws until then leave this room walking or crawling; it's up to you."

She released her hold, but not before pushing her towards the door.

"Get out."

"No, I'll prove I'm the rightful queen."

Lydia witnessed slimy darkness pouring off her as it transformed into a red-eyed cobra. It quickly went to strike when Lydia felt a rush of power overwhelm her and instantly grabbed the monster by the throat.

"What are you doing? Destroy her!"

Lydia stared at the monster as a rainbow aura covered it before shrinking it to the size of an ant.

Without moving her gaze away from Lamia, she stomped on the snake, hearing the satisfying crunch of the snake's demise.

Lamia screamed in utter agony as the dead snake turned to ash before collapsing, barely conscious.

"Ichigo, please help me."

Ichigo moved closer to Lamia, kneeled, and said, "Don't worry, it'll be okay."

Lydia closed her fists as he tenderly touched the woman's hair before taking out what looked like a hairpin with a thin vial.

Ichigo's eyes narrowed to unnerving slits as Lamia's body curled as if trying to hide from his gaze.

"What the heck is that?" Lydia said.

"A cobra's pin."

"Cobra's pin?"

"It's a pin that can carry any poison or potion, especially a love potion."

"You can tell what type it is?"

"I was trained to detect different concoctions, especially ones that are forbidden."

Lamia weakly grabbed his pants and said, "Forgive me, I love you so much that—"

"Enough, guards!"

The guards arrived and bowed as Ichigo said, "Take this woman to the dungeon. I'll deal with her later."

Lamia's eyes widened, and she said, "No, please, I beg you, don't do this!"

The glare from Lamia left a chill down her spine, but she knew it would be a problem to appear shaken.

Lydia boldly met the glare with her own and said, "You can't blame anyone but yourself."

"I'll destroy you, mark my words, Fierce!"

Lydia moved closer until whispering in Lamia's ear, "Come near Ichigo again, and the last beat down will feel like a pet on the head."

"Please, you're all talk."

"There's nothing more dangerous than a black woman who keeps her word."

"Get her out of my sight," screamed Ichigo.

She watched as he snapped the hairpin in two, and tiny embers appeared before it entered Ichigo.

The guards carried the screaming woman out of the room as the sewists entered, bringing multiple beautiful, bright kimonos.

He glanced at her with such intensity that she wanted to fan herself.

"Lydia, I'll be back; the seamstresses will help you."

"Where are you going?"

"I need to prepare for the ceremony."

Ceremony? Oh, for the *New Year.*

"But this is your bedroom."

"I have more than one."

She looked away, knowing a redness was appearing on her cheeks.

"Do I need to bring anything?"

Ichigo moved closer, and his familiar scent left a heated desire so hot it would be a miracle to douse.

"You're the only requirement, my queen."

He admitted before staring at her while holding her hand and kissing it.

Ichigo grinned before leaving as if he hadn't started a lust bonanza.

As the seamstress and her maid measured and found the perfect outfit, she stared at the closed doors.

The tattoo on her shoulder heated as images of his naked upper body popped into her mind, and ideas on how to make him yell her name.

You've created the spark, don't blame me for the wildfire. Lydia thought as she perused the outfits.

I FINALLY REMEMBER her!

He went to another bed chamber and found the clothes for the ceremony carefully laid out on the bed.

The memories flooded back into his mind as soon as he snapped the hairpin. Shame and anger flooded his mind as his past actions resurfaced, causing the ground to shake.

Leaning on his training, he calmed down as the tattoos burned from his emotions.

"Wiseman!"

Instantly, the Wiseman appeared wearing a red attire fitting for his station and said, "Yes, my king."

"How did you find Lydia?"

"Your blood."

"What?"

"When that woman Lamia arrived claiming she was your mate, something didn't sit right with me." "So I used my powers and discovered she was a fraud while your true mate was still out there."

"She had the mark of the snakes."

"Enchanted."

"Why?"

"The enemy's leader desired the zodiac jewel and thought to use Lamia to attain it."

"I assume you've gotten the necessary information from Lamia."

"Yes, it didn't take much."

"What else did you find?"

"It seems the leader knew of Your Majesty's fleeting memory of your mate and used that to his advantage."

"How did they know about Lamia?"

"She crossed the leader by trying to steal from him and was about to torture her."

"Aren't her parents wealthy?"

He remembered that her father was a school board member, while her mother worked as a nurse in a high-end hospital.

"The father had a car accident, leaving him disabled, while the mother was sued for abuse of funds."

"Okay, does she know the leader's location?"

"He erased his location from her mind."

"Typical."

"But she said he was close."

The thirst for revenge raged inside him, but Lydia's smile tempered his anger. He knew she was upset with him, despite her manners, and he was determined to make amends for his mistakes.

"Good, does he know we're onto him?"

"No, Your Majesty."

"Good."

"What are you going to do?"

"You're the Wiseman."

"True, but you're the king, so I follow your orders."

Ichigo stared at the man who had advised him since training and helped him adjust to being king.

"He doesn't know about my memories returning, so let's keep it this way."

"What about Lydia?"

After all those years, the hurt he caused her was still fresh, but he focused on the safety of her and his people.

"She will stay in the dark as well."

"Yes, your majesty."

Ichigo gave a subtle glare, saying, "You took a huge risk moving the jewel from this land."

"It paid off."

"Too risky, don't do it again."

The wiseman bowed as he stared in his reflection. He decided long ago to cut his hair and abandoned the earring. Ichigo's face was more muscular and had a small stubble.

The only difference is that his eyes were dark brown instead of his normal hazel ones.

"As a wise man, I would advise you to fix your relationship with her."

"I don't know where to begin."

"Start by telling her about the ceremony."

"I'll tell her afterward."

"Your majesty, it's imperative to let her know."

"It's too late now."

He entered the bathroom and changed into his red royal attire, which had the markings of a double-golden snake on its coat.

"I pray you know what you're doing," said the wise man with a concerned expression.

"Everything will be fine, she loves me."

I NEVER THOUGHT I WOULD be wearing a red dress for this occasion.

But she figured since it's a celebration and a tradition to wear red, she went with the flow. She asked what the celebration was about, but the ladies giggled as if she had said the funniest thing in the world.

Lydia knew it was only a matter of time before the gate to this world closed, and she needed to find a way to help Ichigo recover his memories.

The ladies led her to an enormous place where various people stood on the side and watched as she ascended onto the golden altar.

She saw the zodiac jewel floating and glowing in the middle of the altar, where Ichigo stood, powerful and majestic, in a matching red outfit that fit him deliciously.

When his gaze landed on her, a fierce throbbing started from her heart down to her womanhood. The snake tattoo on her shoulder seems to cry out for him, which is terrifying yet natural, the closer she comes to him.

Once standing in front of him, she looked into his eyes for any shred of recognition and found a cold glare.

The wise man/ vendor appeared, wearing a golden kimono with a gentle smile, saying, "Welcome everyone as we celebrate the unification of the zodiac jewel, bringing to life the kingdom."

"My king, do you return the jewel?"

"Yes," Ichigo replied without moving his gaze from Lydia.

"My queen, do you return the jewel?"

"I do."

She's glad that the nightmare is almost over as the Wiseman spoke in Japanese with great depth, resulting in anticipation from her.

Applause resounded around the place as the Wiseman held the jewel before covering it with both hands and opening it to reveal a twin. The jewels levitated from his hands before splitting into Ichigo's and Lydia's bodies.

Immediately, she felt her body becoming hot and cold simultaneously while the familiar rainbow surrounded her and Ichigo. It was amazing as the colors flowed around them, as if giving their blessing, and then, quickly, the jewels exited them.

Swirling around the couple, the jewels fused into one and showcased in a succession of each zodiac animal. As quickly as it levitated, the jewel lowered itself into the wise man's hands.

"Xīn hūn kuài lè!"

The crowd mirrored the phrase in unison, which Lydia assumes is a celebration of bringing the jewel back.

Now, I need to help Ichigo with his memories of me and return home.

But for some reason, her body wasn't listening to her brain; it was burning like lava in the Sahara Desert.

She was dizzy from the heat when Ichigo's cool touch brought her back, which didn't help when he whispered, "Do you want help to cool off?"

"I won't do it."

"Why?"

She was struggling not to groan as he nibbled her neck before answering, "We're not married."

"I forgot to tell you something."

Lydia inhaled as his finger privately teased her bosom, struggling to say, "What?"

"We're married."

What!?

"You don't mean..."

"You're officially mine, Mrs. Morimoto."

Chapter 6

He summoned his power to transform into a dragon and grinned as Lydia's eyes widened.

The yelp from her was cute as he picked up her body and flew them to the hot spring of the kingdom.

The wind blowing against him was another reminder that he was free, and a roar of victory was heard.

"Ichigo, where are you taking me?" Lydia hollered with a moan as he softly gripped her body.

It felt like an eternity as the temple roof came into view, and once they entered the forest and then the entrance, he helped Lydia to her feet.

Lydia turned to stare at him with a mixture of desire and anger as he returned to human form.

"Where are we?"

He slowly walked towards her, casting a shadow over her entire vision.

The sensitivity was excruciating as the wind caressed his skin, and he knew it was torturous for Lydia.

"Does it matter right now?"

"Damn you."

He could see the lust glazing over her eyes and knew it was only a matter of time.

"Lydia, I won't force you to do this." "If you wish to wait, then so be it."

The glare intensified from her eyes, but in a surprise twist, she reached and wrapped her arms around his head.

"Be gentle, ok?"

Once those words came from her lips, everything became a blur as he carried her to the room while conquering her with a kiss. He thanked his lucky stars that she was back in his arms again.

The fragrant oil on her skin appealed to his senses as she moaned while rubbing her hands against his skin.

Mate! Take Mate!

He grappled with his animals while laying her down on the bed and witnessed her position as a willing sacrifice.

She's willing! Take her!

No, it's her first time.

She will feel only pleasure, take her!

"Ichigo, I'm so hot!" Lydia whimpered.

Ecstasy coursed through him as she raked her nails against his chest and lower before grabbing both her hands.

"Not yet."

"Ichigo, don't play with me."

He gave a dry chuckle before saying, "I'm not, but I want this to last."

"Oh?"

She raised her hips against his, making an animalistic growl erupt from him.

"Temptress, are you sure you're not using magic?"

"I don't need it."

With ease, he raised her hands above her head and gave a few pecks against her neck, making Lydia squirm.

"Do you trust me?"

Lydia's eyes met his as the desire became unbelievably hotter before she said, "Yes."

Piece by piece, her clothing fell away from her, as if shedding to reveal new skin, and the results were breathtaking.

The soft glow of the candles seemed to magnify her beauty, accentuating her oiled mocha skin, generous breasts, coily, long hair, and tempting lips.

She's perfect and mine.

He gripped her hands with one of his own and descended to his main prize.

"What are you doing, Ichigo?"

"Shhh, I'm exploring."

"Wait, I don't know if I....oh!"

He lightly blew at her womanhood with ease and smiled at her response.

"Is this okay?"

She nodded fervently before tasting to find complete heaven in the form of pineapples and cherries. The more he tasted her essence, the wider he opened her legs for easier access. He grabbed her thighs to keep her in place to continue his feast as she lifted her hips.

"So delicious, so perfect."

He released her hands to feel the stinging sensation of her hand pulling at his scalp. The sounds emanating from her were priceless, pushing him to ring every last one of them out of her.

Gently, he inserted his finger inside her and moved in and out until she met his rhythm.

"Can you take another finger, baby?"

"Yeah, I think so."

"Good."

He entered another finger and crooked it to find her G-spot as Lydia cried out in rapture.

"More, Ichigo."

"Are you sure?"

Her tightened thighs answered him, and he placed another finger inside her until she panted.

Images of her in different positions were moving around in succession as Lydia's response became more than fantasy.

He pumped with little self-control while continuing to taste until tremors from her thighs told him she was close.

He moved faster before taking her pearl into his mouth and sucking.

"Ichigo, I'm..."

"Come."

She screamed so loud that if the heavens were fragile, they would crumble into starry dust from the sky.

Ichigo devoured every drop from her until her muscles relaxed in his arms. He moved up to her body and kissed her on the forehead.

"Good girl."

Lydia's eyes were half-mast and glazed over with pleasure as he rose to align himself with her womanhood.

Soft gongs echoed across the room, stimulating his skin and his manhood harder.

"Are you ready?"

He touched her quivering skin, wet to the touch, and hunger overwhelmed him as he took the same finger and tasted it.

"Ichi..."

"Mine."

The gongs became louder, echoing against his soul and zodiac animals.

With ease, he entered himself inside her as her inner flesh adjusted before holding it captive.

"Ah!"

"So tight."

He waited in difficulty as she adjusted to his size before wiggling her hips.

She wrapped her arms around his neck as he slowly exited from her warmth before impaling her again.

A sync of moans and groans in tune with the gongs as the slow joining becomes slapping flesh.

A heat inside of his soul blazed hotter and molten as her center trapped him as she screamed in abandon.

Finally! Our mate is home!

"I'm coming again!"

"Let's come together, baby."

He lifted her soft, thick body closer to his before pistoning into her warmth in urgency. Sweet scratches embedded deep on his back from her nails as he felt her womb.

"Ichigo, yes, yes."

"You're mine, Lydia." "Forever, mine!"

Light flashed behind his eyes as he released inside her, and her eyes rolled backward as she came.

Must mark her!

Feeling his canines elongate with anticipation, he kneaded her butt before piercing her while inserting his venom.

"Ichigo!"

Lifting his head, the taste of her blood enlarged his manhood, holding them both in place, and the vibrations from the gongs intensified their joining.

"Mine, you're mine!"

"Please, I can't take any more."

"Just one more baby, one more!"

He didn't know who was louder, him or his animals, but it shook the entire room as Lydia's screams of ecstasy matched his roar before lying on the bed, sweaty, tired, and satisfied.

His manhood released its hold on her walls as it became normal before tortuously taking it out. A shiver coursed through them both after the withdrawal, and he lay beside her with a grin, pulling at his lips.

"Wow," she says, smiling.

Pride bloomed in his chest as she lay on the bed, content and relaxed.

"I assume you approve?"

"Yes, I do."

"Good because we have 11 hours to go."

Lydia widened her eyes as he rose from the bed to retrieve water from the dresser.

"What?"

"I forgot to mention that throughout this night, each of my animals will have a turn with you."

"Animals?"

"It's not what you think; we will perform a move representing each zodiac animal."

Cool, pure water moved into his mouth as his strength replenished.

"But I'm exhausted, how can I...ah!"

He walked towards the bed before cradling her in his embrace.

"Drink."

She narrowed her eyes before accepting the water between her lips.

Immediately, Lydia's body shivers receded, and her body became brand new.

"Amazing."

"It's special from the river."

"It can come in handy for those in need."

He shivered as she moved to nip his chest before licking his nipple.

"I thought you were tired."

"Not anymore, besides, I'm curious to know what moves we're going to try out."

Instinctively, he knew his eyes had changed from her expression, but he didn't expect a gentle palm to caress his face.

"Aren't you afraid?"

"As I said before, Ichi, I'm not afraid of you."

"Lydia..."

"Despite everything, I've never stopped..."

He watched as she squirmed in abandon as the familiar heat surrounded them.

"You've never stopped, what, Lydia?"

Even though he knew the answer, it didn't stop him from desiring to hear it.

"My body is hot again..."

He growled as he sensed his animal's anticipation for hours of mating and moved her body on top of his.

"Let me ease it for you."

THE HEAT SEARING HER body was beyond sensational, but when he placed her on top of his toned body, it was magma.

"What do you want me to do?"

"My bride, take what you desire."

A shiver coursed through her as he gathered her hand into his and kissed it.

"I don't know how..."

"Follow your instincts."

She didn't know, but an image of her moving against him in ecstasy had her automatically taking his manhood.

The smoothness of his skin that entered her before twitched to life as she moved it.

"Lydia..."

She watched in fascination as it grew larger, using her hands to carefully position him at her center.

"Shh, my turn."

She lowered herself until she felt unbelievably full in this new position.

With small movements, she could tell from his expressions of ecstasy that she was doing something right.

The subtle vein rubbed so well inside as she increased the pace for more pressure.

"That's it, baby, ride me!"

His hands rubbed and pushed on her butt for more friction before she knew it, lights flashed behind her eyes.

"Ahh!!"

"Lydia!!!"

She gasped as he raised her off and laid her back against the silk sheets, opening her legs to lie between.

Ichigo's manhood groaned from him and her as he ground against her pearl, having her struggling for air. She could swear that he had gotten bigger as he twisted his hips, having her opening wider for more.

"Oh my God....!"

His lips stole her scream as they moved against the silk until the sounds of slapping flesh echoed in the room.

Lydia gazed at his glowing golden gaze while his hair covered their expressions like a waterfall.

She crossed her legs to bring him closer until the familiar pressure became overwhelming.

They screamed in unison as Ichigo still moved inside her.

"Ichigo, I'm sensitive..."

"Good, you have another orgasm to give."

The gongs echoed, vibrating their bodies, and his manhood swelled again as he pierced her shoulder in succession.

"Ahhh!!!"

She placed her hand on his neck as he licked the mark on her neck before roaring his release.

He didn't move for a minute as the swelling deflated, leaving a hollow feeling in her chest before pulling out.

She lay against the feathered pillow as he rose from the bed to retrieve a towel, then moistened it before returning to bed.

Gently, the cool towel touched her heated skin, cleaning her body.

A sigh escaped her lips, resulting in his stopping and saying, "Am I hurting you?"

"No, I never thought you would take care of me during all of this."

A rough finger touched her chin and lifted it to meet his eyes, "You're my wife; therefore, part of me."

"I thought it would be a hit-it-and-quit."

Her heart quickened as he grinned, revealing the subtle fangs of a viper.

Ichigo's hair lay on his shoulders as water, sharp eyes that stared straight into the soul, a honed broad chest, and legs. But in between his legs was enough to have her wanting to drink a gallon of the water from the glass pitcher.

How did that enter me?

"Do you want to wait longer before continuing the ritual?"

A light laugh came out of her, and she said, "Nah, I'm sure you have other moves that you would like to try."

"Maybe, but it'll be up to you."

"Why are you always saying the right things?"

He shrugged, saying, "It's the animals in me."

"Not you?"

A comfortable silence fell over the room as he gazed at her, then took and kissed her hand.

She inhaled as his eyes glowed, "Just let me know when you're ready."

This is going to be a long night, she thought, squeezing her thighs.

Chapter 7

Old urine and crap assaulted her nostrils as she waited inside the pitful cell.
One job I had to do, and it's all ruined because of that bitch, Lydia!

Shivers ran through her body as the groaning sounds of the others around were aggravating.

The plan was simple: to infiltrate the land, seduce the king using a potion, become queen, apprehend the zodiac jewel, and give it to the magical maniac.

She desired to stay alive and have Ichigo's heart, so she agreed to the deal with the magical freak.

Once learning about the magical world, she allowed the warlock to place those slithering serpents on her shoulder.

The power was excellent, and she hungered for more. The warlock promised more once getting the jewel. Afterward, once a fully grown and handsome Ichigo saw her again, she slipped a love drug into a beverage.

Instantly, he fell in love with her, screaming from the rooftops and admitting to her about what he was while being a king.

He brought her to his kingdom, lavishing her with fine clothes and jewelry that couldn't be *found* anywhere else on the planet. She had hit the jackpot, but Wiseman had always been suspicious.

Although Ichigo announced she was his fated mate, she wasn't allowed near the jewel until the wedding ceremony. She bided her time and gave intel to the boss, but when the wedding preparations had finished, the jewel vanished.

It hindered the wedding and Ichigo from officially being powerful.

She would've absorbed his power and attained anything her heart desired.

Then, after a few days, the missing jewel was found, and along with it, Ichigo's true fated mate, Lydia.

Lydia had been a thorn in her side since high school, being a smarty-pants and taking Ichigo's attention away from her. Of all the guys who desired to know and seduce her, she wanted the one who wasn't interested.

Ichigo was perfect for her, knew it from the start, but a certain nerd was always in his shadow like a parasite.

But now she's stuck in this hellhole and without any power.

She'll pay for this!

Heavy footsteps echoed in the jail, and she expected another interrogation to be in her future. An eerie shadow overwhelmed the cell, and she gritted her teeth.

"I don't have anything else to say, so leave me alone."

"Are you sure?"

She widened her eyes at the being, staring with a white smile and a tilt of his head.

"How did you find me?"

"It wasn't hard, but I see you're in a predicament."

Ignoring the wet hay underneath her feet, she went on her hands and knees.

"Please forgive me!"

"Rise, I have a task for you to make up for it."

Relief coursed through her, and she said, "Anything."

"Find the jewel and take it out of the kingdom."

Anxiety and fear rolled into her mind as scenarios of what might happen if caught.

"But..."

"Do it or deal with me."

A soft clink resounded in the hallway before a whining screech of the open cell door signified the dire situation.

The Wizard quietly advanced into her space as chill and sweat leaked from her cheek.

"I'll do it."

"Good girl."

THE CEREMONY FELT LIKE a triathlon as she lay on the bed with a purr coming from her mouth.

If this is a deep, wet dream, don't let me wake up yet.

Ichigo was sleeping next to her with a serene expression, and a grin emerged on her lips.

She had never imagined the first time having sex would be with him, but was glad.

Without thinking, Lydia lightly moved aside loose hairs from his face when his hand caught hers.

"What are you doing?"

"Admiring the view."

"I'm surprised you're awake."

"I drank some water, so don't worry."

"It's too late, aside from the kingdom, you're my priority."

A twinge in her stomach tightened, but she mentally shook it off.

"Is that all?"

"What are you looking for me to say?"

"I wish you could remember us."

"Us, huh?"

"Yes, despite our last encounter, it was a decent friendship."

Ichigo's hand lightly ran his hand down her, "Maybe it's best to leave the past behind, Nv Wang."

How does he remember my nickname? Does he remember?

Lydia's ears perked up, and she said, "Why?"

"Because it's easy to get lost there and harder to move forward in the future."

"How about this, Ichi, we tell each other about ourselves and leave it in the past."

"Sounds fair."

"I'll even tell you my favorite position afterward."

His eyebrows rose at that reward, and he smiled.

"Fine, what do you want to know?"

The conversation took them from how Ichigo's first year of zodiac training was hell to Lydia's hobby of jewelry making became a career. They laughed at the stories and learned small things about each other.

"I can't believe you've done it."

"It was a dare, but I had to clean the shrine for a month."

"Ouch."

"It taught me a valuable lesson."

"What?"

"Don't get caught, especially by a rat shifter."

"So, how long can we stay here?"

"Normally, for two weeks, but we need to finish the New Year before the portal closes for another year."

"What can I do?"

"The queen's responsibility is to help replenish us to control our animals."

"How?"

"The zodiac jewel. It not only keeps our people from suffering but will bestow fortune."

"Sounds easy enough, but what happens if it doesn't happen?"

"Suffering, chaos, and destruction as the shifters won't be able to control their animal and be stuck in an unnerving state."

"Okay, afterward?"

"The citizens will light lanterns, have parades, and serve sweet balls along with the feast.

"Sounds amazing."

"It'll be memorable with you in my arms."

A twinge of guilt affected her happiness as she didn't know how to tell him about her leaving.

I'll tell him after the festivities.

THE NIGHT COULDN'T have been more perfect if he tried, as they snuggled together.

It was like the good Lord above had given him another chance with her and told him not to blow it.

He knew the Wiseman could handle the celebration details, but wanted Lydia to celebrate with him. In the past, as their friendship grew, they became curious about each other's culture.

Lydia would smile as she introduced the traditions in her family, especially one where the girls had to cook every Sunday.

He's surprised that a gut didn't form from all the food her family had given him. But considered her soul food officially part of his top five. In return, he introduced her to various activities of his culture.

Although he knew Lydia's parents were good people and protective of their daughter, he was concerned when introducing her to his parents, who were in grade school.

It shocked him as they welcomed Lydia with open arms and practically adopted her. They would invite her to their weekly dinners and holidays, and the way she embraced the culture was terrific.

"You know, Ichigo, even though your memory of me is gone, I'm glad we can make new ones."

He flinched as her words floated around his ear, and the sincerity warmed his heart.

"I'm glad too."

I'm sorry, Lydia, but until I find the warlock, I have to keep you in the dark.

"Are you okay, Ichi?"

The scent of rosemary and mint caressed his senses, and he kissed the top of her lovely curly hair.

"I'm alright, rest, we have a busy schedule."

Chapter 8

The festival was in full swing as everyone gathered around the kingdom. Lanterns shone in the houses, shrines, and the palace while shifters across the globe came to see the new king and queen.

Ichigo selfishly wanted to keep Lydia's presence away from the others, but brought her back for the ceremony. The traditional New Year attire for royals was white, but they dressed like citizens to learn about their needs.

He could see the task was nerve-wracking for Lydia, but she never showed it. She assumed her role as queen with wisdom and common sense, thanks to the Wiseman's guidance; it was a success.

The only thing left was to use the zodiac jewel to replenish the shifter's strength for the year. He had sent his Wiseman to get it as Lydia walked away from the children.

"How was it?" he asked.

"It was wonderful; the kids proudly showed me their zodiac animals."

"It seems you're settling in."

"I'm trying."

A look of understanding crossed between them as he gathered her hand in his and gave a feathered kiss against her knuckles. A smile touched his lips as her pulse quickened like a hummingbird.

"You're splendid."

He frowned as the time drew late and sent a servant to find the Wise Man. The servant returned with a worried expression as he whispered into his ear.

"Your Highness, the Wiseman, and the jewel are missing, and this was left."

The servant handed him a note demanding that the king and queen come or risk endangering the lives of the shifters.

Rage flowed in his veins as he stared at a familiar person wearing a particular red kimono.

Lamia!

She caught his gaze and grinned as she flowed through the sea of people, disappearing.

He heard Lydia curse as she took the note and said, "What are you waiting for? We need to get them both back."

"We can't."

"What do you mean?"

"You know this is a setup."

"We can't just do nothing."

"I understand that, but as King, I can't leave my people."

"We can protect the people and save him."

"How?"

Her mind was turning as her eyes widened, and she said, "I've got an idea. I'll need a few things."

THE CITY LIGHTS SHONE as Lydia and Ichigo walked around Tokyo Bay until they found the boat where Lamia stood, looking out at the view. Lydia would have grabbed the heifer by the hair, but she kept her focus on the task.

She tightened the jewel in her palm as they boarded, and Lamia's hands gave two loud claps. Red lanterns brightened and appeared around them, hovering over the sea.

"It took you long enough," Lamia said.

"Cut the crap, where's the Wiseman?"

"So hasty, Lydia, aren't you concerned about the jewel?"

"It's not you I'm concerned about since you can't even touch it."

"Oh?"

"Who freed you, Lamia?" Ichigo said with a glare.

"Someone is very anxious to meet you."

"You're wasting my time."

"You don't think you're getting away with this?"

"I already am, Ichi, if you had only stayed with me."

Lamia moved seductively towards Ichigo and reached to touch him when Lydia snatched her wrist.

"Touch my husband and die," Lydia said.

"Please, just because he has his fun doesn't mean it's serious, ugh!"

Lamia flinched as she tightened her hold, feeling satisfaction as the bones felt about to snap.

"Ms. Fierce, this is highly irregular behavior from you."

Lydia sucked in her breath as her assistant revealed himself wearing a black hooded cloak.

Bernie!?

Lamia went to stand next to him with a mocking smile when he touched her on the shoulder.

"You've done well, Lamia."

"Thank you."

"Your debt is settled, now leave."

Lamia was leaving the boat as the lanterns brightened, blinding her eyes. It dimmed, revealing a cow in Lamia's place.

"What the ...?" Lydia demanded.

"I wanted to erase the idea of escape. Lamia needed to pay for her idiocy."

"It wasn't your call."

Bernie sighed as he checked his watch and said, "Now that's settled, please follow me."

Here goes nothing. Lydia thought.

She followed with Ichigo by her side as Lamia's moo echoed into the night.

THE SHIP REVEALED A luxurious platform with a long island, couches near the window, and his wife holding a martini glass.

"Lydia, I'm so glad you could make it."

"Didn't have much choice, Gabriella."

"Semantics."

"Where is he?" Lydia said.

"Hanging around here."

Small sounds resounded in the room until Ichigo gazed at a small Wiseman inside a glass lantern.

"You're the one who planned all this, the head warlock?" Ichigo said as small shadows crept closer to the lantern.

"It's head *witch*, and yes, I hoped that fool Lamia could grab the jewel without trouble, but that Wiseman of yours left a handy failsafe."

"A member of royal blood or their mate could touch the jewel."

"King gets three points, so I'll need you to summon the jewel or witness your wiseman torn to pieces by my shadows."

"Why are you doing this?" Lydia said.

Gabriella rolled her eyes and said, "Ask your husband since he banished my kind from the land."

"You've tortured my people with your curses for sport!"

"And since then, my people died out, barely surviving from a magic depletion."

"So now you want revenge."

"Oh, revenge is the cherry on top, I want your people exposed to the mortals and suffer."

"How could you do that?" Lydia demanded.

"I won't repeat myself, ask your husband."

Lydia's heavy gaze aimed at him felt too much to bear, and he said, "The jewel not only brings life to the kingdom but helps us control our animals."

"What will happen?"

"We would be unable to control our zodiacs and turn against our wishes."

"But they can't touch it."

"You don't understand that if we don't return to the palace by midnight and blow on the jewel, the people will be exposed."

"Blah, Blah, time is ticking," Bernie said.

"Either you're hallucinating or foolish if you would think I would summon it."

"Tough crowd, then you won't mind bluffing with your people," Gabriella said, grinning.

He stiffened at her comment but kept a poker face.

"I'll do it." Lydia declared.

"Lydia, don't!"

"I knew you were a smart woman."

He watched in disbelief as she moved toward the lantern and lifted her hand.

"Forgive me, Wiseman," Lydia said as the Wiseman widened his gaze.

"Stop!"

"Appear."

A shimmering rainbow surrounded her body as the jewel emerged and landed in her hand.

The animals in him stopped him from snatching the jewel as Lydia blew on it.

"Very good, although it won't work." Gabriella rose from her seat and reached for it.

Lydia fisted the jewel tighter and pushed her, saying, "The Wiseman."

"Always business," she said with a snap of her fingers, banishing the shadows and freeing him.

The lantern sparked before crumbling into dust, and with it, a regular-sized Wiseman appeared.

"Lydia, what have you done?" The Wiseman said.

"Saving you."

"My life is a mere drop for the sake of the kingdom."

"Don't disrespect me, now leave."

"Your Highness, why didn't you stop her?"

A growl emanating from him paused the questioning and said, "Leave now."

A mixture of expressions passed the Wiseman's face, but standing out was sadness.

Dejected, the Wiseman left with his head down, singing a sorrowful song in Japanese.

"Now, the jewel, please," Bernie said, approaching Lydia.

Lydia tossed the jewel to Bernie as the hot stamp of betrayal shook his soul.

"You've got what you wanted, now let us go," Lydia said while gazing into Ichigo's eyes.

"This is a perfect soap opera, but you know we can't let you go."

"You don't need us."

"Lydia, even you're not that foolish," Ichigo said as the shadows emerged from the red lanterns.

"Are you calling me a fool?" Lydia said with widened eyes.

"Look at what you've done: You've given them the tool to destroy our kind!"

"Are you seriously doing this now?"

"We're about to be killed!"

Chilling air enveloped them as Gabriella took the jewel and tightened it, a strong pulse echoing in his heart.

Electric pain pushed him to the floor as Lydia ran to him.

"Ichigo!" Lydia said.

"This is just the beginning, and once you're gone, the kingdom will be at my mercy," Gabriella said as the jewel became white.

"I'm sorry, Ichigo."

"I trusted you."

The shadows crept closer, putting minor cuts on his arms and one on Lydia's face.

"It'll be alright."

"Goodbye, your majesties, I hope you make up in hell," Gabriella said as she and Bernie exited.

Ichigo closed his eyes as the shadows covered his and Lydia's bodies with nasty fangs opening wide to devour them.

"Do you think we're cutting it close?" Ichigo said as she took out an artifact.

"Maybe, but we needed to make it believable."

She opened the artifact and watched as it absorbed the shadows, transforming into pieces of furniture.

"Ok, now we need to get back to the palace."

"No need."

"You gave the witch the zodiac jewel."

"Not really, see what they have is a piece of jewelry from my past design."

"But how? I felt pain in my heart."

"I asked Chika to form a camouflage around the jewel and added some power from the soil of the kingdom, but the pain was from the power I lent it."

"And the real one?"

"Currently, in the Wiseman's cloak."

I love this woman!

"Let's go; our kingdom needs us."

LYDIA KNEW IT WAS A long shot to fool Bernie and his wife, but she took the risk.

The cold air bit into her skin as she held onto Ichigo's dragon form as he rushed to stop them.

It was difficult to track them as the clouds covered the moon, but a shroud of darkness zoomed through the forest as fast as lightning.

"Ichigo, we've got to stop them from crossing the bridge."

He maneuvered them toward the villains as they were about to step near the river.

"We've got you!"

Bernie's eyes widened as Ichigo wrapped his tail around him and threw him against the tree. A satisfying thud of his body lying on the earth, unconscious.

I need to tighten my hiring policies, Lydia thought, jumping off Ichigo's back.

Gabriella narrowed her gaze as Lydia blocked the river and said, "Do you seriously believe you've stopped me?"

"I'm going to say this once: let this go and never return."

She pursed her lips as Gabriella laughed and said, "You don't have the power."

The witch swallowed the jewel and convulsed as her body bent in different directions, her skin turning black while increasing in size.

The wind picked up as she transformed into a demon with six horns and a roar that could chill a person to the bone.

Crap!

Swiftly, the demon went behind, and agonizing pain bloomed as it slashed her back.

It was unbearable as her body refused to move from the wound, and her vision became cloudy.

Lydia struggled and met a pair of black eyes as the demon pounced before Ichigo attacked its blind side. He blew a ring of fire around Lydia and growled as the demon shook it off as if it were nothing.

"Ichigo, I need you to move away from me."

A deep growl from him told her it was out of the question, and she watched as the demon walked through the fire.

Lydia moved her hand inside her pants pocket to take out the artifact. Her blood flow increased as she moved, but she focused on the task.

Ichigo opened its jaws when the demon backhanded him across the opening.

"Ichigo!"

The demon moved toward an unconscious Ichigo when Lydia pressed a hidden button on the artifact.

A hiss could be heard as the familiar shadows emerged from it, and she said, "Hey, Gabriella!"

The demon turned to Lydia as she threw a piece of the demon's hair that had been taken and threw it into the fire.

The shadows moved toward the demon and enveloped it. Screeches and roars echoed as the shadows left nothing behind.

I warned you, witch.

A muffled sound emerged from the fire as Ichigo called her name with a terrified expression.

Don't be afraid, Ichi. I'm okay, she thought as blessed darkness took away her pain.

Chapter 9

Blinding light shone against Lydia's face as she peeked at what looked like the view of Tokyo.

She rose with caution as the last memory was of dying from a bleeding wound surrounded by fire.

Touching her back, she felt nothing but smooth skin.

"I could've sworn I was at death's door."

Ichigo!

"Ichigo, where are you?"

Worry erupted as she looked around, finding herself inside an unfamiliar bedroom.

A shattered sound and heavy footsteps approached the door, and not knowing what to expect, she grabbed the first thing she could: a bat.

The door opened, revealing a frantic Ichigo wearing an apron and holding a pot.

"Lydia, you're alright?"

She jumped off the bed and into his arms as tears flowed down her face.

"You're alright!"

Sandalwood and vanilla wafted into her nostrils as he embraced her and softly kissed her head.

"You're alive."

Ichigo's embrace tightened as she sniffled with tears dampening his shirt.

A comforting silence surrounded them as he led her into a modern kitchen that was enviable.

He moves the chair enough for Lydia to sit and pushes her closer to the table. Ichigo walked towards the oven, and she watched as he fixed breakfast. Fried sausage, eggs, and grilled fish wafted around the kitchen as her stomach growled.

Once he finished cooking, he placed them on the table with ease and sat across from her.

She didn't touch her food as memories plagued her mind.

"Do you want to talk about it?" Ichigo said.

Her hands trembled as she licked her lips and said, "How did I survive?"

"I woke in time to find you lying on the ground, bleeding."

A snap drew her attention to his hand holding chopsticks, and she found one in half.

"And?"

"I took you to the palace and into the healing room. There, the doctor placed you in the sacred water and waited."

"How long?"

"Twenty-four hours."

"What?"

"Your wounds were severe, and I didn't know how long you would remain unconscious."

"And Bernie?"

"He was taken into custody, and they erased his memories of the incident and you."

"Me?"

"I'm sure you don't wish for him to come back for revenge."

She nodded as the heavy lifting seemed to be handled and gave him a grateful smile.

"Thank you."

"Your problems are mine."

"What about Gabriella?"

"Nothing but ash, and don't worry, Lamia returned to normal after Gabriella died."

Her muscles loosened after that as she took a bite of her fish.

"Delicious."

"Thanks, I had practice."

"Alright, where are we?"

"My apartment."

Raising an eyebrow, she looked around the place, which was silver and black.

"Cheerful."

"I don't have time to decorate."

"Ever heard of a designer?"

He grinned, sipping his soup, saying, "I'll look into it."

"Why aren't we in the palace?"

"It disappeared."

"What?"

"The kingdom only appears for the days of the Chinese New Year and afterward disappears until next year."

"What about the people?"

"The citizens of the kingdom stay there, and those who visit leave before the portal closes."

"So, we're back in the real world?"

"Yes, it's what you wanted, right?"

She froze as the words registered and placed the fork down. "Yes, it was."

"You're not going to deny it?"

"It's a waste of words. After you had abducted me, I was willing to do anything."

"Even marry me?"

She sighed at his sharp tone but continued, "Yes, I was determined to marry you, and..."

"And what?"

She narrowed her eyes as his skin turned green, and the atmosphere shifted ominously.

"I believe I've done my part."

"Oh?"

"Yes, since you've regained your memories."

Ichigo's fists trembled, revealing claws as he said, "How long have you known?"

"Your nickname for me."

"Well, since I've regained my memories, what will you be doing?"

"Depends on your answer to this question."

"What?"

"Do you love me?"

"Are you serious?"

"Do you?"

Her heart quickened at his hazel eyes, and anticipation flooded her senses as he moved closer. She wanted him to gather her in his arms and admit his love. Lydia closed her eyes as his warm hand touched her cheek and waited.

"You're my mate."

She flinched at his matter-of-fact words and moved away from his touch.

"Is that it?"

"Yes, what more do you want?"

Ichigo's snake form wanted to burst out judging from the slits of his eyes but she didn't care. Besides, he doesn't have the right to be upset with her.

Tears threatened to fall from her eyes as he stood there like a statue, cold and hard.

"Then we've nothing left to talk about."

She felt sorrow as he marked her, crossing his arms and saying, "I'll make arrangements to take you home."

Despite her desire to run into his arms, she held her ground as he left the kitchen without looking back.

Damn you, Morimoto! She thought as tears flowed freely from her eyes.

THREE WEEKS LATER

The town was lively, and temperatures were warm as she drove towards the jewelry store. Despite dealing with the task of finding a new assistant, her business skyrocketed to a remarkable degree after the Chinese New Year's collection.

She had received numerous requests to work for their companies and was considering the top three.

Once returning home, it seemed nothing had happened in anyone's life except her own. Lydia's mother continued trying to set her up with random guys, but it never worked out.

As much as she tried, Ichigo's face refused to disappear from her mind. She knew it was probably because, in a way, she was a married woman. But never told her or Ichigo's family because of what might have happened.

She had considered asking for a divorce, but the thought made her sick to the stomach.

So this is what it feels like to be stuck in a corner.

Lydia had made it to the store and entered to find it was dark.

She closed her eyes at the blinding lights and saw her business associate wearing an excited smile.

"Jessica, what's this all about?"

She pointed behind Lydia as the familiar scent of Sandalwood and vanilla surrounded her.

A warm sensation from her tattoo confirmed it as she turned to find Ichigo holding a bouquet. He wore a business suit that was tailor-made for him, making her suck her teeth in irritation. Bittersweet feelings stopped her from running into his arms, and she crossed her arms.

"Ms. Fierce, please forgive me, but he was adamant about wanting to meet you and offered to buy my entire catalog."

"Jessica..."

"Please, for the sake of our business arrangement, hear him out, but don't worry if he steps out of line, I've got a surprise."

Lydia sighed as the image of Jessica's gun aimed at Ichigo left an uncomfortable ache.

"We'll talk later," Jessica said as she exited to the back.

He moved closer before she raised her hand and said, "What are you doing here?"

"I'm asking for two minutes of your time, that's all."

"Why should I?"

She watched his subtle gulp, answering, "I know I don't deserve it, but please."

The genuine pleading softened her, and she gave him a slight nod, to which he exhaled in relief.

Don't be relieved yet, Morimoto.

He placed the bouquet on the glass case and said, "I've been an ass."

"Yep."

"And after you've left, I was miserable and couldn't function."

"Is it because we're mates?"

He shook his head and covered her hands in his, "I thought it was because of our bond, but it was more than that."

"How?"

"I was taught to be unyielding not just as a warrior but as a man, yet when you came into my life, it brought softer feelings."

Lydia's hand tightened on her sleeve, but she kept silent as he continued.

"It conflicted with what I was, and instead of learning, I cut them down, looking at them as weakness. I thought you were my weakness, so I kept you away."

She looked away momentarily before feeling his soft lips against her hands, "Ichigo…"

"But I should've known that you were my strength and backbone to help me be a better man. What I'm trying to say is I'm sorry and will work for your forgiveness until my dying breath."

Lydia's eyes flooded with tears as his head bowed onto their joined hands.

"Why are you doing this to me, Ichigo?"

"Because I love you, Lydia Fierce, and will prove it every day."

She opened her hands and covered them on his face to discover wetness against her hands.

"You're crying."

He tried to move away, but she kissed each tear on his cheek.

"Lydia…"

"I love you, Ichigo, and I'll hold you to your promise."

"I give my word."

"Actions speak louder, Morimoto."

He kneeled in her presence, continuing to hold her hand, and said, "Then consider this my first act."

She widened her eyes as he revealed the little open blue box and saw a finely cut diamond ring.

"Lydia Rain Fierce, will you marry me again?"

Emotion choked her as he stared at her with open vulnerability and love, nodding. "Yes.

A beautiful smile covered his face as he slid the ring on her finger, saying, "Perfect fit for my queen."

A WOMAN WATCHED THE scene, smiling as the Wiseman appeared from the air.

"I thought I said not to do that."

The Wiseman bowed, saying, "My apologies, you said you needed to see me."

"I had wanted to know about the kingdom and how it's doing."

"The kingdom is in harmony with the zodiac jewel, and the people are safe."

The woman nodded as she watched her son carrying Lydia, kissing and holding her as a precious treasure.

"Your majesty, why did you have me lie to Lydia about you and the king's position?"

"I knew she would've found a way to return and had us help, so a small lie was needed."

"When will you tell them that you and his majesty's memories are indeed intact?"

Ichigo's mother tilted her head before saying, "Maybe after seeing my first grandchild."

"Does His Majesty know about your matchmaking?"

"I don't know what you're talking about. All I know is my son is happy, and the kingdom is safe."

"A new start?"

"A new beginning."

The End

Chapter 10
Epilogue

The wedding planning was a whirlwind, from announcing it to her family and Ichigo's family to being bombarded with magazines and ideas for the location, food, and more.

Lydia smiled as she stared at herself in the mirror. The wedding dress featured a lovely lace chiffon that flowed down her body.

It seemed unbelievable as she prepared to walk down the aisle, with her mother happy and handling the small details.

Lydia and Ichigo separately told their mothers of their 'eloping,' which didn't sit well with either of them.

"I don't know what possessed you to marry him without a wedding," Lydia's mother said, placing a penny in a shoe.

"It was the spur of the moment," Lydia said as she applied a shade of rouge on her lips.

"I'm so happy for you. You deserve so much happiness; I hope to find a love like this," Jessica said.

Be careful what you hope for, Jessica.

"Amazingly, Ichigo managed to get this church at such a short time," Lydia's mother said.

"My son has a knack for negotiation," Mrs. Morimoto said, holding a cherry blossom.

Aside from being a king, Ichigo is a private mogul of a business company that went public not too long ago.

Lydia knew he was intelligent, but to know his accomplishments made her glow with pride.

"Alright, baby, I need to talk to the wedding coordinator," Lydia's mother said, barely containing her tears.

"Ah, none of that, I worked too hard on her makeup - let's go," Jessica said while gently leading them out of the room.

Mrs. Morimoto appeared behind Lydia with a serene expression and smiled. "You look lovely."

"Thank you, Mrs. Morimoto." "Enough of that, call me Mother or Okasan."

"I haven't had a chance to apologize about -"

"You're my son's mate, and I've loved you like a daughter, so no apology needed."

Gently, she placed a cherry blossom on the side of her hair, enhancing her beauty.

Fighting her tears, Lydia said, "Thank you, Mom." The scent of jasmine calmed her as they exchanged a loving hug.

"Hey, I want to join," said Jessica as she entered with a pout.

"I know I'm not missing a hug from my daughter," Mrs. Fierce said.

Lydia laughed as they joined in, and a warm tear slid down her cheek.

"I love you, guys."

ICHIGO STOOD AT THE end of the altar with his heart pounding in his chest.

The wise man, as his best man beside him, said, "Breathe, Ichigo, you should be used to this."

"Whatever."

He had faced various enemies that threatened him to the point of death, but the New Year's wedding was the scariest moment of his life.

Why did I decide to do this again?

The doors opened to reveal an angel approaching him with a smile, offering him his answer.

Lydia's wedding dress was molded in all the right places, her rouge lips glistening and dark brown eyes open with trust.

After the pastor spoke his peace, he gave them room for their vows.

Ichigo spoke from his heart, "Lydia, I knew you were the one for me, from our growing friendship to high school." he continued, "Despite how I ended our relationship, you gave me another chance. I vow to be the man that you need and deserve, forever."

He could hear the sounds of awws and sniffles, but only had eyes for her. The soft quiver of her lips and quick inhalation were worth it.

"Ichigo, I had given up love, and when you came back into my life, it felt as if God was punishing me."

He flinched from the memories but felt her hands tighten in his. "But despite what had transpired between us, we came together stronger than ever. I knew after what happened, I couldn't imagine my life without you. I love you, Ichigo Morimoto. And I vow to be your helpmate and always in your corner."

His throat closed with emotion at her vow, and he softly kissed her hands. "I have nothing else to say, but allow me to introduce Mr. and Mrs. Morimoto."

He quickly grabbed and meshed her against his body and kissed her with all the passion in his heart.

"I love you, Mr. Morimoto."

She groaned as he moved his hand onto her breast, privately kneading and flicking her nipple until it stood at attention."

"Ichigo," she gasped.

"I love you, Mrs. Morimoto."